This book is to be returned on or before
the last date stamped below.

For Alan with best wishes.

Published in Great Britain in 2001 by Hodder Wayland,
an imprint of Hodder Children's Books

Text copyright © 2001 Margaret Nash
Illustrations copyright © 2001 Gini Wade

The right of Margaret Nash to be identified as the author of
this Work and the right of Gini Wade to be identified as the
illustrator of this Work has been asserted by them in accordance
with the Copyright, Designs and Patents Act 1988.

British Library Cataloguing in Publication Data
Nash, Margaret, 1939-
Into the unknown: the Tudor explorers John and Sebastian
Cabot. - (Historical storybooks)
1.Cabot, John, ca.1450-ca.1499 - Juvenile fiction
2.Cabot, Sebastian - Juvenile fiction 3.North America
- Discovery and exploration - Juvenile fiction 4.Historical
fiction 5.Children's stories
I.Title II.Wade, Gini
823.9'14[J]

ISBN 0 7502 3395 8

Printed in Hong Kong by Wing King Tong Co. Ltd.

Hodder Children's Books,
A division of Hodder Headline Limited,
338 Euston Road,
London NW1 3BH

INTO THE UNKNOWN

The Tudor Explorers John and Sebastian Cabot

Margaret Nash

Illustrated by Gini Wade

an imprint of Hodder Children's Books

John and Sebastian Cabot

1496 Henry VII granted John Cabot and his sons permission to sail the seas in search of new lands. At this time many people still believed the world was flat.

1497 The journey of the *Matthew* took place. Cabot thought he had found China, but he had in fact discovered Newfoundland on the north-east coast of America. On his return to England, John Cabot was given the title of Grand Admiral.

1498 John Cabot set sail again but was not seen to return. Many supposed he was lost at sea. Sebastian was the second of John Cabot's three sons. He did indeed become cartographer to the King of England, and led further expeditions under Henry VII and Henry VIII.

1502 Cod was discovered off the coast of Newfoundland, the fishery was started, and trade began.

1544 Sebastian Cabot produced a famous map of the world, now held in Paris.

1997 To mark the five hundredth anniversary of Cabot's voyage, a British crew sailed a replica of the *Matthew* to Newfoundland. This replica ship can be seen by the public at Bristol docks.

Chapter 1
Into the Unknown

Sebastian Cabot leaned against the harbour wall and took a deep breath of salty air. Men were loading the last barrels of fresh water from wooden sleds to the ship. Already the Mayor of Bristol had arrived, wearing his gold chains, and the quayside was full of Bristol merchants, come to see them off on the evening tide.

It was only a year since King Henry had given Father licence to sail across unknown seas to the Orient, but it seemed longer. He'd kept praying to the Lord to make this day come quickly.

'Hey ho!' Sebastian turned and saw his friend crouched behind a barrel. He ran over.

'Edmund, what brings you here?'

'Come to say goodbye. Take care not to fall off the edge of the world, Seb.'

Sebastian laughed, and pushed his friend, who sprawled on the ground grinning, '…and mind you don't get eaten by a sea monster!' A bugle blared, over by the counting house. Men came running from the side streets.

'I must go, Edmund.' Edmund scrambled up, and the two of them, serious for once, shook hands solemnly.

'Remember, keep a journal Seb.'

'I will,' said Sebastian, and ran towards the ship. He took a last look at it from the ground. Although only small, its three masts cut proudly into the evening sky. He ran on deck and waved to Edmund until a priest stepped forward. The priest held up his cross and said a prayer for the *Matthew*. Father was untying the ropes. They were off at last, into the exciting unknown, to find silks and spices in faraway places.

To the shouts and cheers of the crowd,
the *Matthew* was tugged down the Severn
estuary by hoffler boats. In a few hours
they would reach the sea, the rowing boats
would be untied, and up would go the
linen sails.

Sebastian gazed up at the starry sky.

'There'll be no time for staring up there,' said the man beside him. He nudged Sebastian sharply. 'I hope you realize, Master's Son, how hard you're going to have to work on this voyage.'

'Oh yes, Sir.'

'Well mind you do. There's only eighteen of us, heed.' Sebastian remembered the barber-surgeon from the meetings at his father's house. He'd seldom smiled, but Father had said he was good with a knife, and could cut off a limb as easily as he could shave off a beard.

'The dog star is bright tonight,' said a tall sailor, moving towards them. Sebastian agreed. They talked about the constellations until Sebastian couldn't stop yawning.

'I'm going to my bed,' he said. 'Father expects me up at break of day.'

'The Master expects you up,' corrected his father, suddenly appearing. Sebastian held out his hand.

'Good night Master.'

'Good night.'

Chapter 2
No Time to Waste

Sebastian was scrubbing the deck when the grey dawn broke over the sea. He looked up as a pair of boots kicked through the slopping water in front of him.

'Huh! Did you sleep well then, Master's Son?' It was the barber.

'Well enough, Sir.' Sebastian glanced away. He'd spent the first night near Father's cabin. From now on he would sleep up on deck with the others.

A bell rang. Prayers!

Sebastian concentrated hard on the chaplain's words, for God's help was much needed, if they were to discover the north-west passage to the East, and return safely. He sang the hymn heartily, watching the ship rock gently, under its billowing sails.

'God be praised,' shouted his father. 'I think this weather is a good omen.'

Spirits were high, the breakfast was good, and ale flowed freely.

'Give us a tune on your pipe, Musician,'
said the carpenter.

But John Cabot prodded him sharply.
'Time enough for that in the evening. It
would be wiser for you to check that the
leathers on the pumps are good, Carpenter,
and that no seams in the planking are
opening up.' He clapped his hands. 'Every
man to his work.'

Sebastian knew Father wanted no time
wasted. The merchants of Bristol had paid
for the *Matthew* to be built, but Father was
paying for everything else himself.

As Sebastian lay back on his bed-roll under the night stars, he resolved to begin his journal the next day. He looked up at the crow's nest tilting with the ship. Its height would impress his friend Edmund, but Sebastian was not looking forward to taking his turn on watch up there.

Chapter 3
A Nasty Surprise

The days were passing. Already they had left Ireland far behind and were out in the Atlantic Ocean. Sebastian had sneaked below deck into Father's cabin, to write his journal. He dipped the quill in the inkwell. 'So far we've been favoured by God. No pirates. Good progress, and clement weather.'

Pirates were his worst fear. They were mainly in the Mediterranean seas, but Father said they could be anywhere. Although Sebastian often disagreed with Father, John Cabot was to be respected for his seafaring knowledge.

Sebastian reached for the dividers and stood over the chart which was spread across the sea chest. He made a stab where he thought they might be today.

'One day, I shall be cartographer to the King of England,' he said loudly. Then he grinned, sat down and wrote it in his journal. 'And I shall be the greatest explorer that ever lived,' he wrote.

Suddenly the ship lurched. Sebastian staggered. Another lurch sent him reeling into the corner. Sebastian knew about sudden changes in winds. He stumbled along the hold.

'Give me patience!' yelled the cook, who was trying to stir the evening's stew on top of the fire box. Sebastian passed him and heaved himself up through the hatch to the deck, where the men were struggling to fold in the mainsail.

'Amen!' said the priest. 'Now trust in the Lord that the wind will change back to a mild north-easterly soon.'

'Where's Starry?' someone shouted. The men looked at one another. They dashed to the sides. Fear shot through Sebastian. Not his friend who knew the heavens so well. Pray he wasn't overboard. They'd never see him in these churning waters.

'Sebastian, search below,' boomed Father. Sebastian dropped through the hatch to the hold of the ship. Starry was lying on the floor.

He dragged the man, who obviously had
a fever, into Father's cabin, and seconds
later the barber came in.

'Get the bleeding bowl,' he ordered, and
Sebastian obeyed. He watched the barber
let blood from a vein in Starry's arm, then
smear his arm with honey, and bind it.

Sebastian stayed with his friend. He gave him tea, laced with valerian, and watched as the sailor fell asleep. Then he went to get his journal. This incident was worth writing down. He reached out for the quill and stared in horror. The diary had gone!

Chapter 4
The Lost Journal

Sebastian could not find his journal. It was not on the chest, nor on the floor, and Father had not seen it.

'Seek better things to do, Sebastian,' he said severely, and Sebastian spoke no more about it.

By the next day the wind had subsided, and the hot June sun was sparkling the water. Sebastian sat with the others mending sails, and enjoying the movement of the ship and the creaking of the ropes.

'And how is the future cartographer to the King of England then?' Sebastian looked up and saw the barber towering above him. He felt his cheeks flame. The barber brought the journal from behind his back. 'That's what he says about himself, this modest Master's Son. Royal cartographer, no less!'

Sebastian snatched at the journal, but
the barber swung it out of reach, and the
men laughed. He flicked it in Sebastian's
face. 'He tells us he will be the greatest
explorer that ever lived.' The men jeered
and guffawed. 'That's from a lily-livered
boy who's scared to go up the rigging!'

Sebastian winced. He thought no one knew of his fear, for he always took his turn at climbing. The barber read more. 'He tells us…'

Suddenly the carpenter grabbed the journal. 'He tells us nothing. That is a private journal.' The barber hit out but missed.

'Stop your peevishness, you ill-tempered scoundrel!'

The barber spat at him. He grabbed him round the neck and would have thrown Chippie against the mast, but John Cabot was suddenly in their midst.

'Stop grappling like tinkers. Or, make no mistake, I'll have the pair of you strung up.'

Sebastian took the journal. Then a bell rang, meaning the sand glass needed turning, and it was his turn to go on watch. The anger in him made him bold, and for once he climbed the rigging like a monkey.

Sebastian tried to forget his shame. He knew his imagination sometimes took charge of him. Father had accused him more than once of being a dreamer.

He settled his mind on earlier explorers. They must also have watched similar leagues of endless sea. He thought of Marco Polo, the Venetian who'd travelled to China over two hundred years ago, then dear Mother, at home in Bristol. She was Venetian, and lastly of Father, who, though born in Genoa, had earned himself Venetian citizenship, and had read Marco Polo's wonderful account of his voyages. Sebastian took the journal out of his pocket, and hurled it. He watched it go down, down, down, into the sea.

Chapter 5
Danger!

The days were long and melting into one another – with the same routines. Most days they ate stock fish. Weevils had got into the sacks of grain and the ship's biscuits. Sebastian was sick of the hard dry biscuits. He longed for some fresh fruit.

'We're lucky the rats haven't ruined more food,' said Saltbag, busy kneading the day's bread dough. 'And we still have plenty of ale.' He took a swig from the tankard beside him.

Sebastian picked up the cross-staff and put it to his eye, to measure the angle of the sun against the horizon, and work out the northerly position of the boat. The climate was much colder now. There were monstrous icebergs around, some reaching fathoms down into the water. And they made horrible groaning noises. One touch of them could rip the *Matthew* apart. Pray God they would soon find land. He said a quick heartfelt prayer, asking that he might be the first to spot it.

'LAND! LAND!'
The carpenter was
shouting from the
crow's nest – hanging
out, and pointing to the
shape on the horizon.
Sebastian couldn't
believe it. But Chippie
was swinging down the
rigging, and everyone
was throwing things
and cheering.

Father shoved them all aside. He was up in the crow's nest in seconds, and looking into the distance. Looking, and saying nothing. Where were they? Sebastian couldn't wait to find out. China maybe! Then Father was waving his arm widely and shaking his head.

'Clouds, just clouds. No land.' Everyone quietened. You could feel the dismay. The sea took on a grey gloom, the day dimmed, and those wicked clouds got blacker and blacker. There was a storm approaching. They dropped anchor.

The wind was noisy now, the sea was swelling, and the clouds hung like a black lid over them. The men did everything they could, lowered the mainsail, battened down the two hatches, then one of the smaller sails stuck.

Sebastian could see the corner had somehow twisted round the end of the beam, but the men were still tugging. Walls of water crashed over them. They were not looking up. Waves were rising, ten times the height of a man. If the sail ripped who knew what would happen!

Without thinking of his safety, Sebastian clambered onto the rigging. The front of the ship thrust out of the water. Then, as it plunged, a sheet of water hit him and took his breath, but as it rose again he managed to get level with the twisted sail.

'STOP!' Urgency strengthened Sebastian's voice, and the men below stared in amazement. They obeyed. As the ship plummeted again, Sebastian twisted his legs into the ropes, gripped the sail with both hands and forced it off the beam.

He grabbed the ropes again. Then, with the wind battering at him, and his legs shaking, he climbed down. At last he felt the wet, but solid, deck beneath him, and hands there to help him. But as he reached for them, his feet slipped under him. He was flying towards the foredeck. CRASH! His head banged and he felt nothing.

Chapter 6
The New Found Land

Sebastian opened his eyes. Why was he in
Father's cabin? How long had he slept
there? He stood up, clasping his throbbing
head, then shuffled along the hold.

'Hey, good day!' It was Saltbag. He
shouted to the others, who came flocking.

'You fell and hurt your head, Sebastian.
You've been unconscious for two days.'

'A brave lad you were, in that storm.'
Sebastian stared at them.

'What storm?'

The barber was patting his shoulder, and
apologizing for ever thinking ill of him.

Saltbag handed him a bowl of broth,
and while he drank it, the others told him
what had happened, but he could
remember none of it.

'And there's land out there, Sebastian! Real land now,' said Father. 'Can you hear the birds calling?'

'Let me see.' Sebastian, helped by the others, climbed out of the hatch.

There was land all along the horizon.
A flash of disappointment, that God hadn't
answered his prayer, hit Sebastian. He'd
so wanted to be the first to see the new
country. But then, as he looked up the
rigging, the memory of the storm flooded
back. God had had other plans for him
and he'd fulfilled them. He was proud.

There was a striking sunset that evening, with the red sun sinking through its shawl of red and gold clouds. Pipes were played, as the ale jug went from one to the other. He and Starry sat against the foredeck and talked of heavens and oceans, and of all the places there might be to discover in this new, round world. Tomorrow Father would choose a landing place.

Sebastian could see the lines of trees in the distance, getting nearer and nearer, as he watched Father sink the lead-line overboard, to see how deep the water was. When he hauled it up John Cabot found sand on the base of the weight. There was more cheering and whistling. It was hard to believe that, after thirty-five days at sea, they were landing here on 24 June – John the Baptist's day.

'A fine site,' said Father as they sailed into a sandy bay. 'Bona Vista, I shall call it.'

Sebastian kicked off his boots, and wriggled his toes in the fine sand. 'Could there be people, Father?' John Cabot shrugged.

'We should raise the flags of the faith, and the King's standard at once,' he said. And, without further ado, the flags were unfurled and placed in a high spot.

'Thanks be to God,' prayed the chaplain, and led them all in singing a psalm.

Saltbag produced a feast of fresh fish, that evening. There were many toasts to their king, their country, and themselves. Tomorrow they would set sail down the coast, then soon back to England with the news. Sebastian smiled. He would make a map, and decorate it with fish, for the seas were full of codfish. Perhaps one day he really might be cartographer to the King of England!

Glossary

barber-surgeon a man who would cut hair and beards, amputate limbs, and attend to minor medical matters

bed-roll a portable roll of bedding

bleeding bowl Tudor doctors believed that bleeding a person could cure many illnesses; the bowl was used to collect the blood

cross-staff a wooden navigational instrument, shaped like a crossbow

crow's nest the little basket-like cage at the top of the mainsail where a crew member kept watch

dividers a type of compass with two pointed arms, used for measuring lines on maps

fire box a metal container, like a brazier, in which wood was burned for cooking

hoffler boats rowing boats which tugged the sailing ships until they were out at sea

lead-line a lead weight suspended on a line and sunk to find out the depth of water

ship's biscuits a bread-like substance, made from very hard baked wheat and barley

stock fish fish, such as cod, which was split and dried in the air so it would last a long time

valerian a calming herb used to settle the stomach and help bring on sleep

weevils small beetles which eat their way into sacks of grain and food